Marx Joyce Abbott Machiavelli Chesterton Emerson Hardy Montaigne Cooper Austen Defoe Melville Haggard Hugo Eliot Grimm Stoker Carroll Christie Molière Wilde Maupassant Byron Schiller Engels Garnett Einstein Fitzgerald Hawthorne Smith Kafka Goethe Dostoyevsky Hall Cotton Baum Kipling Doyle Willis Leslie Dumas Henry Nietzsche Flaubert Turgenev Balzac Stockton Vatsyayana Crane Burroughs Verne Curtis Tocqueville Whitman Gogol Vinci Homer Widger Tolstoy Busch Darwin Thoreau Scott Potter Freud Zola Twain Plato Lawrence Kant Jowett Stevenson Dickens Andersen Harte London Descartes Cervantes Burton Hesse Poe Aristotle Wells Voltaire Hale James Hastings Cooke Bunner Shakespeare Richter Chambers Irving Doré Swift Dante Chekhov da Shaw Wodehouse Benedict Alcott Pushkin Newton

The Lives of the Twelve Caesars, Volume 05: Claudius

Gaius Suetonius Tranquillus

Imprint

This book is part of TREDITION CLASSICS

Author: Gaius Suetonius Tranquillus
Cover design: Buchgut, Berlin – Germany

Publisher: tredition GmbH, Hamburg - Germany
ISBN: 978-3-8424-6287-8

www.tredition.com
www.tredition.de

The intention of the TREDITION CLASSICS series is to make world literature in the public domain available in printed format. Literary enthusiasts and organizations, such as Project Gutenberg, worldwide have scanned and digitally edited the original texts. tredition has subsequently formatted and redesigned the content into a modern reading layout. Therefore, we cannot guarantee the exact reproduction of the original format of a particular historic edition. Please also note that no modifications have been made to the spelling, therefore it may differ from the orthography used today.

THE LIVES OF THE TWELVE CAESARS

By
C. Suetonius Tranquillus;
To which are added,

HIS LIVES OF THE GRAMMARIANS, RHETORICIANS, AND POETS.

The Translation of
Alexander Thomson, M.D.

revised and corrected by
T.Forester, Esq., A.M.

TIBERIUS CLAUDIUS DRUSUS CAESAR. [465]

(295)

I. Livia, having married Augustus when she was pregnant, was within three months afterwards delivered of Drusus, the father of Claudius Caesar, who had at first the praenomen of Decimus, but afterwards that of Nero; and it was suspected that he was begotten in adultery by his father-in-law. The following verse, however, was immediately in every one's mouth:

Tois eutychousi kai primaena paidia.

Nine months for common births the fates decree;
But, for the great, reduce the term to three.

This Drusus, during the time of his being quaestor and praetor, commanded in the Rhaetian and German wars, and was the first of all the Roman generals who navigated the Northern Ocean [466]. He made likewise some prodigious trenches beyond the Rhine [467], which to this day are called by his name. He overthrew the enemy in several battles, and drove them far back into the depths of the desert. Nor did he desist from pursuing them, until an apparition, in the form of a barbarian woman, of more than human size, appeared to him, and, in the Latin tongue, forbad him to proceed any farther. For these achievements he had the honour of an ovation, and the triumphal ornaments. After his praetorship, he immediately entered on the office of consul, and returning again to Germany, died of disease, in the summer encampment, which thence obtained the name of "The Unlucky Camp." His corpse was carried to Rome by the principal persons of the several municipalities and colonies upon the road, being met and received by the recorders of each place, and buried in the Campus Martius. In honour of his (296) memory, the army erected a monument, round which the soldiers used, annually, upon a certain day, to march in solemn procession, and persons deputed from the several cities of Gaul performed religious rites. The senate likewise, among various other honours, decreed for him a triumphal arch of marble, with trophies, in the Appian Way, and gave the cognomen of Germanicus to him and his posterity. In him the civil and military virtues were equally displayed; for, besides his victories, he gained from the enemy the Spolia Opima [468], and frequently marked out the German chiefs in the midst of their army, and encountered them in single combat, at the utmost hazard of his life. He likewise often declared that he would, some time or other, if possible, restore the ancient government. In this account, I suppose, some have ventured to affirm that Augustus was jealous of him, and recalled him; and because he made no haste to comply with the order, took him off by poison. This I mention, that I may not be guilty of any omission, more than because I think it either true or probable; since Augustus loved him so much when living, that he always, in his wills, made him joint-heir with his sons, as he once declared in the senate; and upon his decease, extolled him in a speech to the people, to that degree, that he prayed the gods "to make his Caesars like him, and to grant himself as honourable an exit out of this world as they had given him." And not satisfied with inscribing upon his tomb an epitaph in verse composed by himself, he wrote likewise the history of his life in prose. He had by the younger Antonia several children, but left behind him only three, namely, Germanicus, Livilla, and Claudius.

II. Claudius was born at Lyons, in the consulship of Julius Antonius, and Fabius Africanus, upon the first of August [469], the very day upon which an altar was first dedicated there to Augustus. He was named Tiberius Claudius Drusus, but soon afterwards, (297) upon the adoption of his elder brother into the Julian family, he assumed the cognomen of Germanicus. He was left an infant by his father, and during almost the whole of his minority, and for some time after he attained the age of manhood, was afflicted with a variety of obstinate disorders, insomuch that his mind and body being greatly impaired, he was, even after his arrival at years of maturity, never thought sufficiently qualified for any public or private employment. He was, therefore, during a long time, and even after the expiration of his minority, under the direction of a pedagogue, who, he complains in a certain memoir, "was a barbarous wretch, and formerly superintendent of the mule-drivers, who was selected for his governor, on purpose to correct him severely on every trifling occasion." On account of this crazy constitution of body and mind, at the spectacle of gladiators, which he gave the people, jointly with his brother, in honour of his father's memory, he presided, muffled up in a pallium—a new fashion. When he assumed the manly habit, he was carried in a litter, at midnight, to the Capitol, without the usual ceremony.

III. He applied himself, however, from an early age, with great assiduity to the study of the liberal sciences, and frequently published specimens of his skill in each of them. But never, with all his endeavours, could he attain to any public post in the government, or afford any hope of arriving at distinction thereafter. His mother, Antonia, frequently called him "an abortion of a man, that had been only begun, but never finished, by nature." And when she would upbraid any one with dulness, she said, "He was a greater fool than her son, Claudius." His grandmother, Augusta, always treated him with the utmost contempt, very rarely spoke to him, and when she did admonish him upon any occasion, it was in writing, very briefly and severely, or by messengers. His sister, Livilla, upon hearing that he was about to be created emperor, openly and loudly expressed her indignation that the Roman people should experience a fate so severe and so much below their grandeur. To exhibit the opinion, both favourable and otherwise, entertained concerning him by Augustus, his great-uncle, I have here subjoined some extracts from the letters of that emperor.

IV. "I have had some conversation with Tiberius, according (298) to your desire, my dear Livia, as to what must be done with your grandson, Tiberius, at the games of Mars. We are both agreed in this, that, once for all, we ought to determine what course to take with him. For if he be really sound and, so to speak, quite right in his intellects [470], why should we hesitate to promote him by the same steps and degrees we did his brother? But if we find him below par, and deficient both in body and mind, we must beware of giving occasion for him and ourselves to be laughed at by the world, which is ready enough to make such things the subject of mirth and derision. For we never shall be easy, if we are always to be debating upon every occasion of this kind, without settling, in the first instance, whether he be really capable of public offices or not. With regard to what you consult me about at the present moment, I am not against his superintending the feast of the priests, in the games of Mars, if he will suffer himself to be governed by his kinsman, Silanus's son, that he may do nothing to make the people stare and laugh at him. But I do not approve of his witnessing the Circensian games from the Pulvinar. He will be there exposed to view in the very front of the theatre. Nor do I like that he should go to the Alban Mount [471], or be at Rome during the Latin festivals. For if he be capable of attending his brother to the mount, why is he not made prefect of the city? Thus, my dear Livia, you have my thoughts upon the matter. In my opinion, we ought to (299) settle this affair once for all, that we may not be always in suspense between hope and fear. You may, if you think proper, give your kinsman Antonia this part of my letter to read." In another letter, he writes as follows: "I shall invite: the youth, Tiberius, every day during your absence, to supper, that he may not sup alone with his friends Sulpicius and Athenodorus. I wish the poor creature was more cautious and attentive in the choice of some one, whose manners, air, and gait might be proper for his imitation:

Atuchei panu en tois spoudaiois lian.
In things of consequence he sadly fails.

Where his mind does not run astray, he discovers a noble disposition." In a third letter, he says, "Let me die, my dear Livia, if I am not astonished, that the declamation of your grandson, Tiberius, should please me; for how he who talks so ill, should be able to declaim so clearly and properly, I cannot imagine." There is no doubt but Augustus, after this, came to a resolution upon the subject, and, accordingly, left him invested with no other honour than that of the Augural priesthood; naming him amongst the heirs of the third degree, who were but distantly allied to his family, for a sixth part of his estate only, with a legacy of no more than eight hundred thousand sesterces.

V. Upon his requesting some office in the state, Tiberius granted him the honorary appendages of the consulship, and when he pressed for a legitimate appointment, the emperor wrote word back, that "he sent him forty gold pieces for his expenses, during the festivals of the Saturnalia and Sigillaria." Upon this, laying aside all hope of advancement, he resigned himself entirely to an indolent life; living in great privacy, one while in his gardens, or a villa which he had near the city; another while in Campania, where he passed his time in the lowest society; by which means, besides his former character of a dull, heavy fellow, he acquired that of a drunkard and gamester.

VI. Notwithstanding this sort of life, much respect was shown him both in public and private. The equestrian (300) order twice made choice of him to intercede on their behalf; once to obtain from the consuls the favour of bearing on their shoulders the corpse of Augustus to Rome, and a second time to congratulate him upon the death of Sejanus. When he entered the theatre, they used to rise, and put off their cloaks. The senate likewise decreed, that he should be added to the number of the Augustal college of priests, who were chosen by lot; and soon afterwards, when his house was burnt down, that it should be rebuilt at the public charge; and that he should have the privilege of giving his vote amongst the men of consular rank. This decree was, however, repealed; Tiberius insisting to have him excused on account of his imbecility, and promising to make good his loss at his own expense. But at his death, he named him in his will, amongst his third heirs, for a third part of his estate, leaving him besides a legacy of two millions of sesterces, and expressly recommending him to the armies, the senate and people of Rome, amongst his other relations.

VII. At last, Caius [473], his brother's son, upon his advancement to the empire, endeavouring to gain the affections of the public by all the arts of popularity, Claudius also was admitted to public offices, and held the consulship jointly with his nephew for two months. As he was entering the Forum for the first time with the fasces, an eagle which was flying that way; alighted upon his right shoulder. A second consulship was also allotted him, to commence at the expiration of the fourth year. He sometimes presided at the public spectacles, as the representative of Caius; being always, on those occasions, complimented with the acclamations of the people, wishing him all happiness, sometimes under the title of the emperor's uncle, and sometimes under that of Germanicus's brother.

VIII. Still he was subjected to many slights. If at any time he came in late to supper, he was obliged to walk round the room some time before he could get a place at table. When he indulged himself with sleep after eating, which was a common practice with him, the company used to throw olive-stones and dates at him. And the buffoons who attended would wake him, as if it were only in jest, with a cane or a whip. Sometimes they would put slippers upon his hands; as he lay snoring, that he might, upon awaking, rub his face with them.

IX. He was not only exposed to contempt, but sometimes likewise to considerable danger: first, in his consulship; for, having been too remiss in providing and erecting the statues of Caius's brothers, Nero and Drusus, he was very near being deprived of his office; and afterwards he was continually harassed with informations against him by one or other, sometimes even by his own domestics. When the conspiracy of Lepidus and Gaetulicus was discovered, being sent with some other deputies into Germany [474], to congratulate the emperor upon the occasion, he was in danger of his life; Caius being greatly enraged, and loudly complaining, that his uncle was sent to him, as if he was a boy who wanted a governor. Some even say, that he was thrown into a river, in his travelling dress. From this period, he voted in the senate always the last of the members of consular rank; being called upon after the rest, on purpose to disgrace him. A charge for the forgery of a will was also allowed to be prosecuted, though he had only signed it as a witness. At last, being obliged to pay eight millions of sesterces on entering upon a new office of priesthood, he was reduced to such straits in his private affairs, that in order to discharge his bond to the treasury, he was under the necessity of exposing to sale his whole estate, by an order of the prefects.

X. Having spent the greater part of his life under these and the like circumstances, he came at last to the empire in the fiftieth year of his age [475], by a very surprising turn of fortune. Being, as well as the rest, prevented from approaching Caius by the conspirators, who dispersed the crowd, under the pretext of his desiring to be private, he retired into an apartment called the Hermaeum [476]; and soon afterwards, terrified by the report of Caius being slain, he crept into an adjoining balcony, where he hid himself behind the hangings of (302) the door. A common soldier, who happened to pass that way, spying his feet, and desirous to discover who he was, pulled him out; when immediately recognizing him, he threw himself in a great fright at his feet, and saluted him by the title of emperor. He then conducted him to his fellow-soldiers, who were all in a great rage, and irresolute what they should do. They put him into a litter, and as the slaves of the palace had all fled, took their turns in carrying him on their shoulders, and brought him into the camp, sad and trembling; the people who met him lamenting his situation, as if the poor innocent was being carried to execution. Being received within the ramparts [477], he continued all night with the sentries on guard, recovered somewhat from his fright, but in no great hopes of the succession. For the consuls, with the senate and civic troops, had possessed themselves of the Forum and Capitol, with the determination to assert the public liberty; and he being sent for likewise, by a tribune of the people, to the senate-house, to give his advice upon the present juncture of affairs, returned answer, "I am under constraint, and cannot possibly come." The day afterwards, the senate being dilatory in their proceedings, and worn out by divisions amongst themselves, while the people who surrounded the senate-house shouted that they would have one master, naming Claudius, he suffered the soldiers assembled under arms to swear allegiance to him, promising them fifteen thousand sesterces a man; he being the first of the Caesars who purchased the submission of the soldiers with money. [478]

XI. Having thus established himself in power, his first object was to abolish all remembrance of the two preceding days, in which a revolution in the state had been canvassed. Accordingly, he passed an act of perpetual oblivion and pardon for every thing said or done during that time; and this he faithfully observed, with the exception only of putting to death a few tribunes and centurions concerned in the conspiracy against Caius, both as an example, and because he understood that they had also planned his own death. He now turned (303) his thoughts towards paying respect to the memory of his relations. His most solemn and usual oath was, "By Augustus." He prevailed upon the senate to decree divine honours to his grandmother Livia, with a chariot in the Circensian procession drawn by elephants, as had been appointed for Augustus [479]; and public offerings to the shades of his parents. Besides which, he instituted Circensian games for his father, to be celebrated every year, upon his birth-day, and, for his mother, a chariot to be drawn through the circus; with the title of Augusta, which had been refused by his grandmother [480]. To the memory of his brother [481], to which, upon all occasions, he showed a great regard, he gave a Greek comedy, to be exhibited in the public diversions at Naples [482], and awarded the crown for it, according to the sentence of the judges in that solemnity. Nor did he omit to make honourable and grateful mention of Mark Antony; declaring by a proclamation, "That he the more earnestly insisted upon the observation of his father Drusus's birth-day, because it was likewise that of his grandfather Antony." He completed the marble arch near Pompey's theatre, which had formerly been decreed by the senate in honour of Tiberius, but which had been neglected [483]. And though he cancelled all the acts of Caius, yet he forbad the day of his assassination, notwithstanding it was that of his own accession to the empire, to be reckoned amongst the festivals.

XII. But with regard to his own aggrandisement, he was sparing and modest, declining the title of emperor, and refusing all excessive honours. He celebrated the marriage of his daughter and the birth-day of a grandson with great privacy, at home. He recalled none of those who had been banished, without a decree of the senate: and requested of them permission for the prefect of the military tribunes and pretorian guards to attend him in the senate-house [484]; and (304) also that they would be pleased to bestow upon his procurators judicial authority in the provinces [485]. He asked of the consuls likewise the privilege of holding fairs upon his private estate. He frequently assisted the magistrates in the trial of causes, as one of their assessors. And when they gave public spectacles, he would rise up with the rest of the spectators, and salute them both by words and gestures. When the tribunes of the people came to him while he was on the tribunal, he excused himself, because, on account of the crowd, he could not hear them unless they stood. In a short time, by this conduct, he wrought himself so much into the favour and affection of the public, that when, upon his going to Ostia, a report was spread in the city that he had been way-laid and slain, the people never ceased cursing the soldiers for traitors, and the senate as parricides, until one or two persons, and presently after several others, were brought by the magistrates upon the rostra, who assured them that he was alive, and not far from the city, on his way home.

XIII. Conspiracies, however, were formed against him, not only by individuals separately, but by a faction; and at last his government was disturbed with a civil war. A low fellow was found with a poniard about him, near his chamber, at midnight. Two men of the equestrian order were discovered waiting for him in the streets, armed with a tuck and a huntsman's dagger; one of them intending to attack him as he came out of the theatre, and the other as he was sacrificing in the temple of Mars. Gallus Asinius and Statilius Corvinus, grandsons of the two orators, Pollio and Messala [486], formed a conspiracy against him, in which they engaged many of his freedmen and slaves. Furius Camillus Scribonianus, his lieutenant in Dalmatia, broke into rebellion, but was reduced in (305) the space of five days; the legions which he had seduced from their oath of fidelity relinquishing their purpose, upon an alarm occasioned by ill omens. For when orders were given them to march, to meet their new emperor, the eagles could not be decorated, nor the standards pulled out of the ground, whether it was by accident, or a divine interposition.

XIV. Besides his former consulship, he held the office afterwards four times; the first two successively [487], but the following, after an interval of four years each [488]; the last for six months, the others for two; and the third, upon his being chosen in the room of a consul who died; which had never been done by any of the emperors before him. Whether he was consul or out of office, he constantly attended the courts for the administration of justice, even upon such days as were solemnly observed as days of rejoicing in his family, or by his friends; and sometimes upon the public festivals of ancient institution. Nor did he always adhere strictly to the letter of the laws, but overruled the rigour or lenity of many of their enactments, according to his sentiments of justice and equity. For where persons lost their suits by insisting upon more than appeared to be their due, before the judges of private causes, he granted them the indulgence of a second trial. And with regard to such as were convicted of any great delinquency, he even exceeded the punishment appointed by law, and condemned them to be exposed to wild beasts. [489]

XV. But in hearing and determining causes, he exhibited a strange inconsistency of temper, being at one time circumspect and sagacious, at another inconsiderate and rash, and sometimes frivolous, and like one out of his mind. In correcting the roll of judges, he struck off the name of one who, concealing the privilege his children gave him to be excused from serving, had answered to his name, as too eager for the office. Another who was summoned before him in a cause of his own, but alleged that the affair did not properly come under the (306) emperor's cognizance, but that of the ordinary judges, he ordered to plead the cause himself immediately before him, and show in a case of his own, how equitable a judge he would prove in that of other persons. A woman refusing to acknowledge her own son, and there being no clear proof on either side, he obliged her to confess the truth, by ordering her to marry the young man [490]. He was much inclined to determine causes in favour of the parties who appeared, against those who did not, without inquiring whether their absence was occasioned by their own fault, or by real necessity. On proclamation of a man's being convicted of forgery, and that he ought to have his hand cut off, he insisted that an executioner should be immediately sent for, with a Spanish sword and a block. A person being prosecuted for falsely assuming the freedom of Rome, and a frivolous dispute arising between the advocates in the cause, whether he ought to make his appearance in the Roman or Grecian dress, to show his impartiality, he commanded him to change his clothes several times according to the character he assumed in the accusation or defence. An anecdote is related of him, and believed to be true, that, in a particular cause, he delivered his sentence in writing thus: "I am in favour of those who have spoken the truth." [491] By this he so much forfeited the good opinion of the world, that he was everywhere and openly despised. A person making an excuse for the non-appearance of a witness whom he had sent for from the provinces, declared it was impossible for him to appear, concealing the reason for some time: at last, after several interrogatories were put to him on the subject, he answered, "The man is dead;" to which Claudius replied, "I think that is a sufficient excuse." Another thanking him for suffering a person who was prosecuted to make his defence by counsel, added, "And yet it is no more than what is usual." I have likewise heard some old men say [492], that the advocates used to abuse his patience so grossly, that they would not only (307) call him back, as he was quitting the tribunal, but would seize him by the lap of his coat, and sometimes catch him by the heels, to make him stay. That such behaviour, however strange, is not incredible, will appear from this anecdote. Some obscure Greek, who was a litigant, had an altercation with him, in which he called out, "You are an old fool." [493] It is certain that a Roman knight, who was prosecuted by an impotent device of his enemies on a false charge of abominable obscenity with women, observing that common strumpets were summoned against him and allowed to give evidence, upbraided Claudius in very harsh and severe terms with his folly and cruelty, and threw his style, and some books which he had in his hands, in his face, with such violence as to wound him severely in the cheek.

XVI. He likewise assumed the censorship [494], which had been discontinued since the time that Paulus and Plancus had jointly held it. But this also he administered very unequally, and with a strange variety of humour and conduct. In his review of the knights, he passed over, without any mark of disgrace, a profligate young man, only because his father spoke of him in the highest terms; "for," said he, "his father is his proper censor." Another, who was infamous for debauching youths and for adultery, he only admonished "to indulge his youthful inclinations more sparingly, or at least more cautiously;" [495] adding, "why must I know what mistress you keep?" When, at the request of his friends, he had taken off a mark of infamy which he had set upon one knight's name, he said, "Let the blot, however, remain." He not only struck out of the list of judges, but likewise deprived of the freedom of Rome, an illustrious man of the highest provincial rank in Greece, only because he was ignorant of the Latin language. Nor in this review did he suffer any one to give an account of his conduct by an advocate, but obliged each man to speak for himself in the best way he could. He disgraced many, and some that little expected it, and for a reason entirely new, namely, for going out of Italy without his license; (308) and one likewise, for having in his province been the familiar companion of a king; observing, that, in former times, Rabirius

Posthumus had been prosecuted for treason, although he only went after Ptolemy to Alexandria for the purpose of securing payment of a debt [496]. Having tried to brand with disgrace several others, he, to his own greater shame, found them generally innocent, through the negligence of the persons employed to inquire into their characters; those whom he charged with living in celibacy, with want of children, or estate, proving themselves to be husbands, parents, and in affluent circumstances. One of the knights who was charged with stabbing himself, laid his bosom bare, to show that there was not the least mark of violence upon his body. The following incidents were remarkable in his censorship. He ordered a car, plated with silver, and of very sumptuous workmanship, which was exposed for sale in the Sigillaria [497], to be purchased, and broken in pieces before his eyes. He published twenty proclamations in one day, in one of which he advised the people, "Since the vintage was very plentiful, to have their casks well secured at the bung with pitch:" and in another, he told them, "that nothing would sooner cure the bite of a viper, than the sap of the yew-tree."

XVII. He undertook only one expedition, and that was of short duration. The triumphal ornaments decreed him by the senate, he considered as beneath the imperial dignity, and was therefore resolved to have the honour of a real triumph. For this purpose, he selected Britain, which had never been attempted by any one since Julius Caesar [498], and was then chafing (309) with rage, because the Romans would not give up some deserters. Accordingly, he set sail from Ostia, but was twice very near being wrecked by the boisterous wind called Circius [499], upon the coast of Liguria, and near the islands called Stoechades [500]. Having marched by land from Marseilles to Gessoriacum [501], he thence passed over to Britain, and part of the island submitting to him, within a few days after his arrival, without battle or bloodshed, he returned to Rome in less than six months from the time of his departure, and triumphed in the most solemn manner [502]; to witness which, he not only (310) gave leave to governors of provinces to come to Rome, but even to some of the exiles. Among the spoils taken from the enemy, he fixed upon the pediment of his house in the Palatium, a naval crown, in token of his having passed, and, as it were, conquered the Ocean, and had it suspended near the civic crown which was there before.

Messalina, his wife, followed his chariot in a covered litter [503]. Those who had attained the honour of triumphal ornaments in the same war, rode behind; the rest followed on foot, wearing the robe with the broad stripes. Crassus Frugi was mounted upon a horse richly caparisoned, in a robe embroidered with palm leaves, because this was the second time of his obtaining that honour.

XVIII. He paid particular attention to the care of the city, and to have it well supplied with provisions. A dreadful fire happening in the Aemiliana [504], which lasted some time, he passed two nights in the Diribitorium [505], and the soldiers and gladiators not being in sufficient numbers to extinguish it, he caused the magistrates to summon the people out of all the streets in the city, to their assistance. Placing bags of money before him, he encouraged them to do their utmost, declaring, that he would reward every one on the spot, according to their exertions.

XIX. During a scarcity of provisions, occasioned by bad crops for several successive years, he was stopped in the middle of the Forum by the mob, who so abused him, at the same time pelting him with fragments of bread, that he had some (311) difficulty in escaping into the palace by a back door. He therefore used all possible means to bring provisions to the city, even in the winter. He proposed to the merchants a sure profit, by indemnifying them against any loss that might befall them by storms at sea; and granted great privileges to those who built ships for that traffic. To a citizen of Rome he gave an exemption from the penalty of the Papia-Poppaean law [506]; to one who had only the privilege of Latium, the freedom of the city; and to women the rights which by law belonged to those who had four children: which enactments are in force to this day.

XX. He completed some important public works, which, though not numerous, were very useful. The principal were an aqueduct, which had been begun by Caius; an emissary for the discharge of the waters of the Fucine lake [507], and the harbour of Ostia; although he knew that Augustus had refused to comply with the repeated application of the Marsians for one of these; and that the other had been several times intended by Julius Caesar, but as often abandoned on account of the difficulty of its execution. He brought to the city the cool and plentiful springs of the Claudian water, one of which is called Caeruleus, and the other Curtius and Albudinus, as likewise the river of the New Anio, in a stone canal; and distributed them into many magnificent reservoirs. The canal from the Fucine lake was undertaken as much for the sake of profit, as for the honour of the enterprise; for there were parties who offered to drain it at their own expense, on condition of their having a grant of the land laid dry. With great difficulty he completed a canal three miles in length, partly by cutting through, and partly by tunnelling, a mountain; thirty thousand men being constantly employed in the work for eleven years [508]. He formed the harbour at Ostia, by carrying out circular piers on the right and on the left, with (312) a mole protecting, in deep water, the entrance of the port [509]. To secure the foundation of this mole, he sunk the vessel in which the great obelisk [510] had been brought from Egypt [511]; and built upon piles a very lofty tower, in imitation of the Pharos at Alexandria, on which lights were burnt to direct mariners in the night.

XXI. He often distributed largesses of corn and money among the people, and entertained them with a great variety of public magnificent spectacles, not only such as were usual, and in the accustomed places, but some of new invention, and others revived from ancient models, and exhibited in places where nothing of the kind had been ever before attempted. In the games which he presented at the dedication of Pompey's theatre [512], which had been burnt down, and was rebuilt by him, he presided upon a tribunal erected for him in the orchestra; having first paid his devotions, in the temple above, and then coming down through the centre of the circle, while all the people kept their seats in profound silence [513]. He likewise (313) exhibited the secular games [514], giving out that Augustus had anticipated the regular period; though he himself says in his history, "That they had been omitted before the age of Augustus, who had calculated the years with great exactness, and again brought them to their regular period." [515] The crier was therefore ridiculed, when he invited people in the usual form, "to games which no person had ever before seen, nor ever would again;" when many were still living who had already seen them; and some of the performers who had formerly acted in them, were now again brought upon the stage. He likewise frequently celebrated the Circensian games in the Vatican [516], sometimes exhibiting a hunt of wild beasts, after every five courses. He embellished the Circus Maximus with marble barriers, and gilded goals, which before were of common stone [517] and wood, and assigned proper places for the senators, who were used to sit promiscuously with the other spectators. Besides the chariot-races, he exhibited there the Trojan game, and wild beasts from Africa, which were encountered by a troop of pretorian knights, with their tribunes, and even the prefect at the head of them; besides Thessalian horse, who drive fierce bulls round the circus, leap upon their backs when they have exhausted their fury, and drag them by the horns to the ground. He gave exhibitions of gladiators in several places, and of various kinds; one yearly on the anniversary of his accession in the pretorian camp [518], but without any hunting, or the usual apparatus; another in the Septa as usual; and in the same place, another out of the common way, and of a few days' continuance only, which he called Sportula; because when he was going to present it, he informed the people by proclamation, "that he invited them to a late supper, got up in haste, and without ceremony." Nor did he lend himself to any kind of public diversion with more freedom and hilarity; insomuch that he would hold out his left hand, and (314) joined by the common people, count upon his fingers aloud the gold pieces presented to those who came off conquerors. He would earnestly invite the company to be merry; sometimes calling them his "masters," with a mixture of insipid, far-fetched jests. Thus, when the people called for Palumbus [519], he said, "He would give them one when he could catch it." The following was well-intended, and well-timed; having, amidst great applause, spared a gladiator, on the intercession of his four sons, he sent a billet immediately round the theatre, to remind the people, "how much it behoved them to get children, since they had before them an example how useful they had been in procuring favour and security for a gladiator." He likewise represented in the Campus Martius, the assault and sacking of a town, and the surrender of the British kings [520], presiding in his general's cloak. Immediately before he drew off the waters from the Fucine lake, he exhibited upon it a naval fight. But the combatants on board the fleets crying out, "Health attend you, noble emperor! We, who are about to peril our lives, salute you;" and he replying, "Health attend you too," they all refused to fight, as if by that response he had meant to excuse them. Upon this, he hesitated for a time, whether he should not destroy them all with fire and sword. At last, leaping from his seat, and running along the shore of the lake with tottering steps, the result of his foul excesses, he, partly by fair words, and partly by threats, persuaded them to engage. This spectacle represented an engagement between the fleets of Sicily and Rhodes; consisting each of twelve ships of war, of three banks of oars. The signal for the encounter was given by a silver Triton, raised by machinery from the middle of the lake.

XXII. With regard to religious ceremonies, the administration of affairs both civil and military, and the condition of all orders of the people at home and abroad, some practices he corrected, others which had been laid aside he revived; and some regulations he introduced which were entirely new. In appointing new priests for the several colleges, he made no appointments without being sworn. When an earthquake (315) happened in the city, he never failed to summon the people together by the praetor, and appoint holidays for sacred rites. And upon the sight of any ominous bird in the City or Capitol, he issued an order for a supplication, the words of which, by virtue of his office of high priest, after an exhortation from the rostra, he recited in the presence of the people, who repeated them after him; all workmen and slaves being first ordered to withdraw.

XXIII. The courts of judicature, whose sittings had been formerly divided between the summer and winter months, he ordered, for the dispatch of business, to sit the whole year round. The jurisdiction in matters of trust, which used to be granted annually by special commission to certain magistrates, and in the city only, he made permanent, and extended to the provincial judges likewise. He altered a clause added by Tiberius to the Papia-Poppaean law [521], which inferred that men of sixty years of age were incapable of begetting children. He ordered that, out of the ordinary course of proceeding, orphans might have guardians appointed them by the consuls; and that those who were banished from any province by the chief magistrate, should be debarred from coming into the City, or any part of Italy. He inflicted on certain persons a new sort of banishment, by forbidding them to depart further than three miles from Rome. When any affair of importance came before the senate, he used to sit between the two consuls upon the seats of the tribunes. He reserved to himself the power of granting license to travel out of Italy, which before had belonged to the senate.

XXIV. He likewise granted the consular ornaments to his Ducenarian procurators. From those who declined the senatorian dignity, he took away the equestrian. Although he had in the beginning of his reign declared, that he would admit no man into the senate who was not the great-grandson of a Roman citizen, yet he gave the "broad hem" to the son of a freedman, on condition that he should be adopted by a Roman knight. Being afraid, however, of incurring censure by such an act, he informed the public, that his ancestor Appius Caecus, the censor, had elected the sons of freedmen into (316) the senate; for he was ignorant, it seems, that in the times of Appius, and a long while afterwards, persons manumitted were not called freedmen, but only their sons who were free-born. Instead of the expense which the college of quaestors was obliged to incur in paving the high-ways, he ordered them to give the people an exhibition of gladiators; and relieving them of the provinces of Ostia and [Cisalpine] Gaul, he reinstated them in the charge of the treasury, which, since it was taken from them, had been managed by the praetors, or those who had formerly filled that office. He gave the triumphal ornaments to Silanus, who was betrothed to his daughter, though he was under age; and in other cases, he bestowed them on so many, and with so little reserve, that there is extant a letter unanimously addressed to him by all the legions, begging him "to grant his consular lieutenants the triumphal ornaments at the time of their appointment to commands, in order to prevent their seeking occasion to engage in unnecessary wars." He decreed to Aulus Plautius the honour of an ovation [522], going to meet him at his entering the city, and walking with him in the procession to the Capitol, and back, in which he took the left side, giving him the post of honour. He allowed Gabinius Secundus, upon his conquest of the Chauci, a German tribe, to assume the cognomen of Chaucius. [523]

XXV. His military organization of the equestrian order was this. After having the command of a cohort, they were promoted to a wing of auxiliary horse, and subsequently received the commission of tribune of a legion. He raised a body of militia, who were called Supernumeraries, who, though they were a sort of soldiers, and kept in reserve, yet received pay. He procured an act of the senate to prohibit all soldiers from attending senators at their houses, in the way of respect and compliment. He confiscated the estates of all freedmen who presumed to take upon themselves the equestrian rank. Such of them as were ungrateful to their patrons, and were complained of by them, he reduced to their former condition of (317) slavery; and declared to their advocates, that he would always give judgment against the freedmen, in any suit at law which the masters might happen to have with them. Some persons having exposed their sick slaves, in a languishing condition, on the island of Aesculapius [524], because of the tediousness of their cure; he declared all who were so exposed perfectly free, never more to return, if they should recover, to their former servitude; and that if any one chose to kill at once, rather than expose, a slave, he should be liable for murder. He published a proclamation, forbidding all travellers to pass through the towns of Italy any otherwise than on foot, or in a litter or chair [525]. He quartered a cohort of soldiers at Puteoli, and another at Ostia, to be in readiness against any accidents from fire. He prohibited foreigners from adopting Roman names, especially those which belonged to families [526]. Those who falsely pretended to the freedom of Rome, he beheaded on the Esquiline. He gave up to the senate the provinces of Achaia and Macedonia, which Tiberius had transferred to his own administration. He deprived the Lycians of their liberties, as a punishment for their fatal dissensions; but restored to the Rhodians their freedom, upon their repenting of their former misdemeanors. He exonerated for ever the people of Ilium from the payment of taxes, as being the founders of the Roman race; reciting upon the occasion a letter in Greek, (318) from the senate and people of Rome to king Seleucus [527], on which they promised him their friendship and alliance, provided that he would grant their kinsmen the Iliensians immunity from all burdens.

He banished from Rome all the Jews, who were continually making disturbances at the instigation of one Chrestus [528]. He allowed the ambassadors of the Germans to sit at the public spectacles in the seats assigned to the senators, being induced to grant them favours by their frank and honourable conduct. For, having been seated in the rows of benches which were common to the people, on observing the Parthian and Armenian ambassadors sitting among the senators, they took upon themselves to cross over into the same seats, as being, they said, no way inferior to the others, in point either, of merit or rank. The religious rites of the Druids, solemnized with such horrid cruelties, which had only been forbidden the citizens of Rome during the reign of Augustus, he utterly abolished among the Gauls [529]. On the other hand, he attempted (319) to transfer the Eleusinian mysteries from Attica to Rome [530]. He likewise ordered the temple of Venus Erycina in Sicily, which was old and in a ruinous condition, to be repaired at the expense of the Roman people. He concluded treaties with foreign princes in the forum, with the sacrifice of a sow, and the form of words used by the heralds in former times. But in these and other things, and indeed the greater part of his administration, he was directed not so much by his own judgment, as by the influence of his wives and freedmen; for the most part acting in conformity to what their interests or fancies dictated.

XXVI. He was twice married at a very early age, first to Aemilia Lepida, the grand-daughter of Augustus, and afterwards to Livia Medullina, who had the cognomen of Camilla, and was descended from the old dictator Camillus. The former he divorced while still a virgin, because her parents had incurred the displeasure of Augustus; and he lost the latter by sickness on the day fixed for their nuptials. He next married Plautia Urgulanilla, whose father had enjoyed the honour of a triumph; and soon afterwards, Aelia Paetina, the daughter of a man of consular rank. But he divorced them both; Paetina, upon some trifling causes of disgust; and Urgulanilla, for scandalous lewdness, and the suspicion of murder. After them he took in marriage Valeria Messalina, the daughter of Barbatus Messala, his cousin. But finding that, besides her other shameful debaucheries, she had even gone so far as to marry in his own absence Caius Silius, the settlement of her dower being formally signed, in the presence of the augurs, he put her to death. When summoning his pretorians to his presence, he made to them this declaration: "As I have been so unhappy in my unions, I am resolved to continue in future unmarried; and if I should not, I give you leave to stab me." He was, however, unable to persist in this resolution; for he began immediately to think of another wife; and even of taking back Paetina, whom he had formerly divorced: he thought also of Lollia

Paulina, who had been married to Caius Caesar. But being ensnared by the arts of Agrippina, (320) the daughter of his brother Germanicus, who took advantage of the kisses and endearments which their near relationship admitted, to inflame his desires, he got some one to propose at the next meeting of the senate, that they should oblige the emperor to marry Agrippina, as a measure highly conducive to the public interest; and that in future liberty should be given for such marriages, which until that time had been considered incestuous. In less than twenty-four hours after this, he married her [531]. No person was found, however, to follow the example, excepting one freedman, and a centurion of the first rank, at the solemnization of whose nuptials both he and Agrippina attended.

XXVII. He had children by three of his wives: by Urgulanilla, Drusus and Claudia; by Paetina, Antonia; and by Messalina, Octavia, and also a son, whom at first he called Germanicus, but afterwards Britannicus. He lost Drusus at Pompeii, when he was very young; he being choked with a pear, which in his play he tossed into the air, and caught in his mouth. Only a few days before, he had betrothed him to one of Sejanus's daughters [532]; and I am therefore surprised that some authors should say he lost his life by the treachery of Sejanus. Claudia, who was, in truth, the daughter of Boter his freedman, though she was born five months before his divorce, he ordered to be thrown naked at her mother's door. He married Antonia to Cneius Pompey the Great [533], and afterwards to Faustus Sylla [534], both youths of very noble parentage; Octavia to his step-son Nero [535], after she had been contracted to Silanus. Britannicus was born upon the twentieth day of his reign, and in his second consulship. He often earnestly commended him to the soldiers, holding him in his arms before their ranks; and would likewise show him to the people in the theatre, setting him upon his lap, or holding him out whilst he was still very young; and was sure to receive their acclamations, and good wishes on his behalf. Of his (321) sons-in-law, he adopted Nero. He not only dismissed from his favour both Pompey and Silanus, but put them to death.

XXVIII. Amongst his freedmen, the greatest favourite was the eunuch Posides, whom, in his British triumph, he presented with the pointless spear, classing him among the military men. Next to him, if not equal, in favour was Felix [536], whom he not only preferred to commands both of cohorts and troops, but to the government of the province of Judaea; and he became, in consequence of his elevation, the husband of three queens [537]. Another favourite was Harpocras, to whom he granted the privilege of being carried in a litter within the city, and of holding public spectacles for the entertainment of the people. In this class was likewise Polybius, who assisted him in his studies, and had often the honour of walking between the two consuls. But above all others, Narcissus, his secretary, and Pallas [538], the comptroller of his accounts, were in high favour with him. He not only allowed them to receive, by decree of the senate, immense presents, but also to be decorated with the quaestorian and praetorian ensigns of honour. So much did he indulge them in amassing wealth, and plundering the public, that, upon his complaining, once, of the lowness of his exchequer, some one said, with great reason, that "It would be full enough, if those two freedmen of his would but take him into partnership with them."

XXIX. Being entirely governed by these freedmen, and, as I have already said, by his wives, he was a tool to others, rather than a prince. He distributed offices, or the command of armies, pardoned or punished, according as it suited their interests, (322) their passions, or their caprice; and for the most part, without knowing, or being sensible of what he did. Not to enter into minute details relative to the revocation of grants, the reversal of judicial decisions, obtaining his signature to fictitious appointments, or the bare-faced alteration of them after signing; he put to death Appius Silanus, the father of his son-in-law, and the two Julias, the daughters of Drusus and Germanicus, without any positive proof of the crimes with which they were charged, or so much as permitting them to make any defence. He also cut off Cneius Pompey, the husband of his eldest daughter; and Lucius Silanus, who was betrothed to the younger Pompey, was stabbed in the act of unnatural lewdness with a favourite paramour. Silanus was obliged to quit the office of praetor upon the fourth of the calends of January [29th Dec.], and to kill himself on new year's day [539] following, the very same on which Claudius and Agrippina were married. He condemned to death five and thirty senators, and above three hundred Roman knights, with so little attention to what he did, that when a centurion brought him word of the execution of a man of consular rank, who was one of the number, and told him that he had executed his order, he declared, "he had ordered no such thing, but that he approved of it;" because his freedmen, it seems, had said, that the soldiers did nothing more than their duty, in dispatching the emperor's enemies without waiting for a warrant. But it is beyond all belief, that he himself, at the marriage of Messalina with the adulterous Silius, should actually sign the writings relative to her dowry; induced, as it is pretended, by the design of diverting from himself and transferring upon another the danger which some omens seemed to threaten him.

XXX. Either standing or sitting, but especially when he lay asleep, he had a majestic and graceful appearance; for he was tall, but not slender. His grey looks became him well, and he had a full neck. But his knees were feeble, and failed him in walking, so that his gait was ungainly, both when he assumed state, and when he was taking diversion. He was outrageous in his laughter, and still more so in his wrath, for then he foamed at the mouth, and discharged from his nostrils. He also stammered in his speech, and had a tremulous motion (323) of the head at all times, but particularly when he was engaged in any business, however trifling.

XXXI. Though his health was very infirm during the former part of his life, yet, after he became emperor, he enjoyed a good state of health, except only that he was subject to a pain of the stomach. In a fit of this complaint, he said he had thoughts of killing himself.

XXXII. He gave entertainments as frequent as they were splendid, and generally when there was such ample room, that very often six hundred guests sat down together. At a feast he gave on the banks of the canal for draining the Fucine Lake, he narrowly escaped being drowned, the water at its discharge rushing out with such violence, that it overflowed the conduit. At supper he had always his own children, with those of several of the nobility, who, according to an ancient custom, sat at the feet of the couches. One of his guests having been suspected of purloining a golden cup, he invited him again the next day, but served him with a porcelain jug. It is said, too, that he intended to publish an edict, "allowing to all people the liberty of giving vent at table to any distension occasioned by flatulence," upon hearing of a person whose modesty, when under restraint, had nearly cost him his life.

XXXIII. He was always ready to eat and drink at any time or in any place. One day, as he was hearing causes in the Forum of Augustus, he smelt the dinner which was preparing for the Salii [540], in the temple of Mars adjoining, whereupon he quitted (324) the tribunal, and went to partake of the feast with the priests.

He scarcely ever left the table until he had thoroughly crammed himself and drank to intoxication; and then he would immediately fall asleep, lying upon his back with his mouth open. While in this condition, a feather was put down his throat, to make him throw up the contents of his stomach. Upon composing himself to rest, his sleep was short, and he usually awoke before midnight; but he would sometimes sleep in the daytime, and that, even, when he was upon the tribunal; so that the advocates often found it difficult to wake him, though they raised their voices for that purpose. He set no bounds to his libidinous intercourse with women, but never betrayed any unnatural desires for the other sex. He was fond of gaming, and published a book upon the subject. He even used to play as he rode in his chariot, having the tables so fitted, that the game was not disturbed by the motion of the carriage.

XXXIV. His cruel and sanguinary disposition was exhibited upon great as well as trifling occasions. When any person was to be put to the torture, or criminal punished for parricide, he was impatient for the execution, and would have it performed in his own presence. When he was at Tibur, being desirous of seeing an example of the old way of putting malefactors to death, some were immediately bound to a stake for the purpose; but there being no executioner to be had at the place, he sent for one from Rome, and waited for his coming until night. In any exhibition of gladiators, presented either by himself or others, if any of the combatants chanced to fall, he ordered them to be butchered, especially the Retiarii, that he might see their faces in the agonies of death. Two gladiators happening to kill each other, he immediately ordered some little knives to be made of their swords for his own use. He took great pleasure in seeing men engage with wild beasts, and the combatants who appeared on the stage at noon. He would therefore come to the theatre by break of day, and at noon, dismissing the people to dinner, continued sitting himself; and besides those who were devoted to that sanguinary fate, he would match others with the beasts, upon slight or sudden occasions; as, for instance, the carpenters and their (326) assistants, and people of that sort, if a machine, or any piece of work in which they had been employed about the theatre did not answer the purpose for which it had been intended. To this desperate kind of encounter he forced one of his nomenclators, even encumbered as he was by wearing the toga.

XXXV. But the characteristics most predominant in him were fear and distrust. In the beginning of his reign, though he much affected a modest and humble appearance, as has been already observed, yet he durst not venture himself at an entertainment without being attended by a guard of spearmen, and made soldiers wait upon him at table instead of servants. He never visited a sick person, until the chamber had been first searched, and the bed and bedding thoroughly examined. At other times, all persons who came to pay their court to him were strictly searched by officers appointed for that purpose; nor was it until after a long time, and with much difficulty, that he was prevailed upon to excuse women, boys, and girls from such rude handling, or suffer their attendants or writing-masters to retain their cases for pens and styles. When Camillus formed his plot against him, not doubting but his timidity might be worked upon without a war, he wrote to him a scurrilous, petulant, and threatening letter, desiring him to resign the government, and betake himself to a life of privacy. Upon receiving this requisition, he had some thoughts of complying with it, and summoned together the principal men of the city, to consult with them on the subject.

XXXVI. Having heard some loose reports of conspiracies formed against him, he was so much alarmed, that he thought of immediately abdicating the government. And when, as I have before related, a man armed with a dagger was discovered near him while he was sacrificing, he instantly ordered the heralds to convoke the senate, and with tears and dismal exclamations, lamented that such was his condition, that he was safe no where; and for a long time afterwards he abstained from appearing in public. He smothered his ardent love for Messalina, not so much on account of her infamous conduct, as from apprehension of danger; believing that she aspired to share with Silius, her partner in adultery, the imperial dignity. (326) Upon this occasion he ran in a great fright, and a very shameful manner, to the camp, asking all the way he went, "if the empire were indeed safely his?"

XXXVII. No suspicion was too trifling, no person on whom it rested too contemptible, to throw him into a panic, and induce him to take precautions for his safety, and meditate revenge. A man engaged in a litigation before his tribunal, having saluted him, drew him aside, and told him he had dreamt that he saw him murdered; and shortly afterwards, when his adversary came to deliver his plea to the emperor, the plaintiff, pretending to have discovered the murderer, pointed to him as the man he had seen in his dream; whereupon, as if he had been taken in the act, he was hurried away to execution. We are informed, that Appius Silanus was got rid of in the same manner, by a contrivance betwixt Messalina and Narcissus, in which they had their several parts assigned them. Narcissus therefore burst into his lord's chamber before daylight, apparently in great fright, and told him that he had dreamt that Appius Silanus had murdered him. The empress, upon this, affecting great surprise, declared she had the like dream for several nights successively. Presently afterwards, word was brought, as it had been agreed on, that Appius was come, he having, indeed, received orders the preceding day to be there at that time; and, as if the truth of the dream was sufficiently confirmed by his appearance at that juncture, he was immediately ordered to be prosecuted and put to death. The day following, Claudius related the whole affair to the senate, and acknowledged his great obligation to his freedmen for watching over him even in his sleep.

XXXVIII. Sensible of his being subject to passion and resentment, he excused himself in both instances by a proclamation, assuring the public that "the former should be short and harmless, and the latter never without good cause." After severely reprimanding the people of Ostia for not sending some boats to meet him upon his entering the mouth of the Tiber, in terms which might expose them to the public resentment, he wrote to Rome that he had been treated as a private person; yet immediately afterwards he pardoned them, and that in a way which had the appearance of making them (327) satisfaction, or begging pardon for some injury he had done them.

Some people who addressed him unseasonably in public, he pushed away with his own hand. He likewise banished a person who had been secretary to a quaestor, and even a senator who had filled the office of praetor, without a hearing, and although they were innocent; the former only because he had treated him with rudeness while he was in a private station, and the other, because in his aedileship he had fined some tenants of his, for selling cooked victuals contrary to law, and ordered his steward, who interfered, to be whipped. On this account, likewise, he took from the aediles the jurisdiction they had over cooks'-shops. He did not scruple to speak of his own absurdities, and declared in some short speeches which he published, that he had only feigned imbecility in the reign of Caius, because otherwise it would have been impossible for him to have escaped and arrived at the station he had then attained. He could not, however, gain credit for this assertion; for a short time afterwards, a book was published under the title of Moron anastasis, "The Resurrection of Fools," the design of which was to show "that nobody ever counterfeited folly."

XXXIX. Amongst other things, people admired in him his indifference and unconcern; or, to express it in Greek, his meteoria and ablepsia. Placing himself at table a little after Messalina's death, he enquired, "Why the empress did not come?" Many of those whom he had condemned to death, he ordered the day after to be invited to his table, and to game with him, and sent to reprimand them as sluggish fellows for not making greater haste. When he was meditating his incestuous marriage with Agrippina, he was perpetually calling her, "My daughter, my nursling, born and brought up upon my lap." And when he was going to adopt Nero, as if there was little cause for censure in his adopting a son-in-law, when he had a son of his own arrived at years of maturity; he continually gave out in public, "that no one had ever been admitted by adoption into the Claudian family."

XL. He frequently appeared so careless in what he said, and so inattentive to circumstances, that it was believed he never reflected who he himself was, or amongst whom, or at (328) what time, or in what place, he spoke. In a debate in the senate relative to the butchers and vintners, he cried out, "I ask you, who can live without a bit of meat?" And mentioned the great plenty of old taverns, from which he himself used formerly to have his wine. Among other reasons for his supporting a certain person who was candidate for the quaestorship, he gave this: "His father," said he, "once gave me, very seasonably, a draught of cold water when I was sick." Upon his bringing a woman as a witness in some cause before the senate, he said, "This woman was my mother's freedwoman and dresser, but she always considered me as her master; and this I say, because there are some still in my family that do not look upon me as such." The people of Ostia addressing him in open court with a petition, he flew into a rage at them, and said, "There is no reason why I should oblige you: if any one else is free to act as he pleases, surely I am." The following expressions he had in his mouth every day, and at all hours and seasons: "What! do you take me for a Theogonius?" [541] And in Greek lalei kai mae thingane, "Speak, but do not touch me;" besides many other familiar sentences, below the dignity of a private person, much more of an emperor, who was not deficient either in eloquence or learning, as having applied himself very closely to the liberal sciences.

XLI. By the encouragement of Titus Livius [542], and with the assistance of Sulpicius Flavus, he attempted at an early age the composition of a history; and having called together a numerous auditory, to hear and give their judgment upon it, he read it over with much difficulty, and frequently interrupting himself. For after he had begun, a great laugh was raised amongst the company, by the breaking of several benches from the weight of a very fat man; and even when order was restored, he could not forbear bursting out into violent fits of laughter, at the remembrance of the accident. After he became emperor, likewise, he wrote several things (329) which he was careful to have recited to his friends by a reader. He commenced his history from the death of the dictator Caesar; but afterwards he took a later period, and began at the conclusion of the civil wars; because he found he could not speak with freedom, and a due regard to truth, concerning the former period, having been often taken to task both by his mother and grandmother. Of the earlier history he left only two books, but of the latter, one and forty. He compiled likewise the "History of his Own Life," in eight books, full of absurdities, but in no bad style; also, "A Defence of Cicero against the Books of Asinius Gallus," [543] which exhibited a considerable degree of learning. He besides invented three new letters, and added them to the former alphabet [544], as highly necessary. He published a book to recommend them while he was yet only a private person; but on his elevation to imperial power he had little difficulty in introducing them into common use; and these letters are still extant in a variety of books, registers, and inscriptions upon buildings.

XLII. He applied himself with no less attention to the study of Grecian literature, asserting upon all occasions his love of that language, and its surpassing excellency. A stranger once holding a discourse both in Greek and Latin, he addressed him thus; "Since you are skilled in both our tongues." And recommending Achaia to the favour of the senate, he said, "I have a particular attachment to that province, on account of our common studies." In the senate he often made long replies to ambassadors in that language. On the tribunal he frequently quoted the verses of Homer. When at any time he had taken vengeance on an enemy or a conspirator, he scarcely ever gave to the tribune on guard, who, (330) according to custom, came for the word, any other than this.

Andr' epamynastai, ote tis proteros chalepaenae.
'Tis time to strike when wrong demands the blow.

To conclude, he wrote some histories likewise in Greek, namely, twenty books on Tuscan affairs, and eight on the Carthaginian; in consequence of which, another museum was founded at Alexandria, in addition to the old one, and called after his name; and it was ordered, that, upon certain days in every year, his Tuscan history should be read over in one of these, and his Carthaginian in the other, as in a school; each history being read through by persons who took it in turn.

XLIII. Towards the close of his life, he gave some manifest indications that he repented of his marriage with Agrippina, and his adoption of Nero. For some of his freedmen noticing with approbation his having condemned, the day before, a woman accused of adultery, he remarked, "It has been my misfortune to have wives who have been unfaithful to my bed; but they did not escape punishment." Often, when he happened to meet Britannicus, he would embrace him tenderly, and express a desire "that he might grow apace," and receive from him an account of all his actions: using the Greek phrase, "o trosas kai iasetai,—He who has wounded will also heal." And intending to give him the manly habit, while he was yet under age and a tender youth, because his stature would allow of it, he added, "I do so, that the Roman people may at last have a real Caesar." [545]

XLIV. Soon afterwards he made his will, and had it signed by all the magistrates as witnesses. But he was prevented from proceeding further by Agrippina, accused by her own guilty conscience, as well as by informers, of a variety of crimes. It is agreed that he was taken off by poison; but where, and by whom administered, remains in uncertainty. Some authors say that it was given him as he was feasting with the priests in the Capitol, by the eunuch Halotus, his taster. Others say (331) by Agrippina, at his own table, in mushrooms, a dish of which he was very fond [546]. The accounts of what followed likewise differ. Some relate that he instantly became speechless, was racked with pain through the night, and died about daybreak; others, that at first he fell into a sound sleep, and afterwards, his food rising, he threw up the whole; but had another dose given him; whether in water-gruel, under pretence of refreshment after his exhaustion, or in a clyster, as if designed to relieve his bowels, is likewise uncertain.

XLV. His death was kept secret until everything was settled relative to his successor. Accordingly, vows were made for his recovery, and comedians were called to amuse him, as it was pretended, by his own desire. He died upon the third of the ides of October [13th October], in the consulship of Asinius Marcellus and Acilius Aviola, in the sixty-fourth year of his age, and the fourteenth of his reign [547]. His funeral was celebrated with the customary imperial pomp, and he was ranked amongst the gods. This honour was taken from him by Nero, but restored by Vespasian.

XLVI. The chief presages of his death were, the appearance of a comet, his father Drusus's monument being struck by lightning, and the death of most of the magistrates of all ranks that year. It appears from several circumstances, that he was sensible of his approaching dissolution, and made no secret of it. For when he nominated the consuls, he appointed no one to fill the office beyond the month in which he died. At the last assembly of the senate in which he made his appearance, he earnestly exhorted his two sons to unity with each other, and with earnest entreaties commended to the fathers the care of their tender years. And in the last cause he heard from the tribunal, he repeatedly declared in open court, "That he was now arrived at the last stage of mortal existence;" whilst all who heard it shrunk at hearing these ominous words.

* * * * * *

The violent death of Caligula afforded the Romans a fresh opportunity to have asserted the liberty of their country; but the conspirators had concerted no plan, by which they should proceed upon the assassination of that tyrant; and the indecision of the senate, in a debate of two days, on so sudden an emergency, gave time to the caprice of the soldiers to interpose in the settlement of the government. By an accident the most fortuitous, a man devoid of all pretensions to personal merit, so weak in understanding as to be the common sport of the emperor's household, and an object of contempt even to his own kindred; this man, in the hour of military insolence, was nominated by the soldiers as successor to the Roman throne. Not yet in possession of the public treasury, which perhaps was exhausted, he could not immediately reward the services of his electors with a pecuniary gratification; but he promised them a largess of fifteen thousand sesterces a man, upwards of a hundred and forty pounds sterling; and as we meet with no account of any subsequent discontents in the army, we may justly conclude that the promise was soon after fulfilled. This transaction laid the foundation of that military despotism, which, through many succeeding ages, convulsed the Roman empire.

Besides the interposition of the soldiers upon this occasion, it appears that the populace of Rome were extremely clamorous for the government of a single person, and for that of Claudius in particular. This partiality for a monarchical government proceeded from two causes. The commonalty, from their obscure situation, were always the least exposed to oppression, under a tyrannical prince. They had likewise ever been remarkably fond of stage-plays and public shows, with which, as well as with scrambles, and donations of bread and other victuals, the preceding emperor had frequently gratified them. They had therefore less to fear, and more to hope, from the government of a single person than any other class of Roman citizens. With regard to the partiality for Claudius, it may be accounted for partly from the low habits of life to which he had been addicted, in consequence of which many of them were familiarly acquainted with him; and this circumstance likewise increased their hope of deriving some advantage from his accession. Exclusive of all these considerations, it is highly probable that the populace were instigated in favour of Claudius by the artifices of his freedmen, persons of mean extraction, by whom he was afterwards entirely governed, and who, upon such an occasion, would exert their utmost efforts to procure his appointment to the throne. From the debate in the senate having continued during (333) two days, it was evident that there was still a strong party for restoring the ancient form of government. That they were in the end overawed by the clamour of the multitude, is not surprising, when we consider that the senate was totally unprovided with resources of every kind for asserting the independence of the nation by arms; and the commonalty, who interrupted their deliberations, were the only people by whose assistance they ever could effect the restitution of public freedom. To this may be added, that the senate, by the total reduction of their political importance, ever since the overthrow of the republic, had lost both the influence and authority which they formerly enjoyed. The extreme cruelty, likewise, which had been exercised during the last two reigns, afforded a further motive for relinquishing all attempts in favour of liberty, as they might be severely revenged upon themselves by the subsequent emperor: and it was a degree of moderation in Claudius, which palliates the injustice of his cause, that he began his government with an act of amnesty respecting the public transactions which ensued upon the death of Caligula.

Claudius, at the time of his accession, was fifty years of age; and though he had hitherto lived apparently unambitious of public honours, accompanied with great ostentation, yet he was now seized with a desire to enjoy a triumph. As there existed no war, in which he might perform some military achievement, his vanity could only be gratified by invading a foreign country, where, contrary to the advice contained in the testament of Augustus, he might attempt to extend still further the limits of the empire. Either Britain, therefore, or some nation on the continent, at a great distance from the capital, became the object of such an enterprize; and the former was chosen, not only as more convenient, from its vicinity to the maritime province of Gaul, but on account of a remonstrance lately presented by the Britons to the court of Rome, respecting the protection afforded to some persons of that nation, who had fled thither to elude the laws of their country. Considering the state of Britain at that time, divided as it was into a number of principalities, amongst which there was no general confederacy for mutual defence, and where the alarm excited by the invasion of Julius Caesar, upwards of eighty years before, had long since been forgotten; a sudden attempt upon the island could not fail to be attended with success. Accordingly, an army was sent over, under the command of Aulus Plautius, an able general, who defeated the natives in several engagements, and penetrated a considerable way into the country. Preparations for the emperor's voyage now being made, Claudius set sail from Ostia, at the mouth of (334) the Tiber; but meeting with a violent storm in the Mediterranean, he landed at Marseilles, and proceeding thence to Boulogne in Picardy, passed over into Britain. In what part he debarked, is uncertain, but it seems to have been at some place on the south-east coast of the island. He immediately received the submission of several British states, the Cantii, Atrebates, Regni, and Trinobantes, who inhabited those parts; and returning to Rome, after an absence of six months, celebrated with great pomp the triumph, for which he had undertaken the expedition.

In the interior parts of Britain, the natives, under the command of Caractacus, maintained an obstinate resistance, and little progress was made by the Roman arms, until Ostorius Scapula was sent over to prosecute the war. He penetrated into the country of the Silures, a warlike tribe, who inhabited the banks of the Severn; and having defeated Caractacus in a great battle, made him prisoner, and sent him to Rome. The fame of the British prince had by this time spread over the provinces of Gaul and Italy; and upon his arrival in the Roman capital, the people flocked from all quarters to behold him. The ceremonial of his entrance was conducted with great solemnity.

On a plain adjoining the Roman camp, the pretorian troops were drawn up in martial array: the emperor and his court took their station in front of the lines, and behind them was ranged the whole body of the people. The procession commenced with the different trophies which had been taken from the Britons during the progress of the war. Next followed the brothers of the vanquished prince, with his wife and daughter, in chains, expressing by their supplicating looks and gestures the fears with which they were actuated. But not so Caractacus himself. With a manly gait and an undaunted countenance, he marched up to the tribunal, where the emperor was seated, and addressed him in the following terms:

"If to my high birth and distinguished rank, I had added the virtues of moderation, Rome had beheld me rather as a friend than a captive; and you would not have rejected an alliance with a prince, descended from illustrious ancestors, and governing many nations. The reverse of my fortune to you is glorious, and to me humiliating. I had arms, and men, and horses; I possessed extraordinary riches; and can it be any wonder that I was unwilling to lose them? Because Rome aspires to universal dominion, must men therefore implicitly resign themselves to subjection? I opposed for a long time the progress of your arms, and had I acted otherwise, would either you have had the glory of conquest, or I of a brave resistance? I am now in your (335) power: if you are determined to take revenge, my fate will soon be forgotten, and you will derive no honour from the transaction. Preserve my life, and I shall remain to the latest ages a monument of your clemency."

Immediately upon this speech, Claudius granted him his liberty, as he did likewise to the other royal captives. They all returned their thanks in a manner the most grateful to the emperor; and as soon as their chains were taken off, walking towards Agrippina, who sat upon a bench at a little distance, they repeated to her the same fervent declarations of gratitude and esteem.

History has preserved no account of Caractacus after this period; but it is probable, that he returned in a short time to his own country, where his former valour, and the magnanimity, which he had displayed at Rome, would continue to render him illustrious through life, even amidst the irretrievable ruin of his fortunes.

The most extraordinary character in the present reign was that of Valeria Messalina, the daughter of Valerius Messala Barbatus. She was married to Claudius, and had by him a son and a daughter. To cruelty in the prosecution of her purposes, she added the most abandoned incontinence. Not confining her licentiousness within the limits of the palace, where she committed the most shameful excesses, she prostituted her person in the common stews, and even in the public streets of the capital. As if her conduct was already not sufficiently scandalous, she obliged C. Silius, a man of consular rank, to divorce his wife, that she might procure his company entirely to herself. Not contented with this indulgence to her criminal passion, she next persuaded him to marry her; and during an excursion which the emperor made to Ostia, the ceremony of marriage was actually performed between them. The occasion was celebrated with a magnificent supper, to which she invited a large company; and lest the whole should be regarded as a frolic, not meant to be consummated, the adulterous parties ascended the nuptial couch in the presence of the astonished spectators. Great as was the facility of Claudius's temper in respect of her former behaviour, he could not overlook so flagrant a violation both of public decency and the laws of the country. Silius was condemned to death for the adultery which he had perpetrated with reluctance; and Messalina was ordered into the emperor's presence, to answer for her conduct. Terror now operating upon her mind in conjunction with remorse, she could not summon the resolution to support such an interview, but retired into the gardens of Lucullus, there to indulge at last the compunction which she felt for her crimes, and to meditate the entreaties by which she should endeavour to soothe the resentment (336) of her husband. In the extremity of her distress, she attempted to lay violent hands upon herself, but her courage was not equal to the emergency. Her mother, Lepida, who had not spoken with her for some years before, was present upon the occasion, and urged her to the act which alone could put a period to her infamy and wretchedness. Again she made an effort, but again her resolution abandoned her; when a tribune burst into the gardens, and plunging his sword into her body, she instantly expired. Thus perished a woman, the scandal of whose lewdness resounded throughout the empire, and of whom a great satirist, then living, has said, perhaps without a hyperbole,

Et lassata viris, necdum satiata, recessit. —Juvenal, Sat. VI.

It has been already observed, that Claudius was entirely governed by his freedmen; a class of retainers which enjoyed a great share of favour and confidence with their patrons in those times. They had before been the slaves of their masters, and had obtained their freedom as a reward for their faithful and attentive services. Of the esteem in which they were often held, we meet with an instance in Tiro, the freedman of Cicero, to whom that illustrious Roman addresses several epistles, written in the most familiar and affectionate strain of friendship. As it was common for them to be taught the more useful parts of education in the families of their masters, they were usually well qualified for the management of domestic concerns, and might even be competent to the superior departments of the state, especially in those times when negotiations and treaties with foreign princes seldom or never occurred; and in arbitrary governments, where public affairs were directed more by the will of the sovereign or his ministers, than by refined suggestions of policy.

From the character generally given of Claudius before his elevation to the throne, we should not readily imagine that he was endowed with any taste for literary composition; yet he seems to have exclusively enjoyed this distinction during his own reign, in which learning was at a low ebb. Besides history, Suetonius informs us that he wrote a Defence of Cicero against the Charges of Asinius Gallus. This appears to be the only tribute of esteem or approbation paid to the character of Cicero, from the time of Livy the historian, to the extinction of the race of the Caesars. Asinius Gallus was the son of Asinius Pollio, the orator. Marrying Vipsania after she had been divorced by Tiberius, he incurred the displeasure of that emperor, and died of famine, either voluntarily, or by order of the tyrant. He wrote a comparison between his father and Cicero, in which, with more filial partiality than justice, he gave the preference to the former.

FOOTNOTES:

[465] A.U.C. 714.

[466] Pliny describes Drusus as having in this voyage circumnavigated Germany, and reached the Cimbrian Chersonese, and the Scythian shores, reeking with constant fogs.

[467] Tacitus, Annal. xi. 8, 1, mentions this fosse, and says that Drusus sailed up the Meuse and the Waal. Cluverius places it between the village of Iselvort and the town of Doesborg.

[468] The Spolia Opima were the spoils taken from the enemy's king, or chief, when slain in single combat by a Roman general. They were always hung up in the Temple of Jupiter Feretrius. Those spoils had been obtained only thrice since the foundation of Rome; the first by Romulus, who slew Acron, king of the Caeninenses; the next by A. Cornelius Cossus, who slew Tolumnius, king of the Veientes, A.U. 318; and the third by M. Claudius Marcellus, who slew Viridomarus, king of the Gauls, A.U. 330.

[469] A.U.C. 744.

[470] This epistle, as it was the habit of Augustus, is interspersed with Greek phrases.

[471] The Alban Mount is the most interesting feature of the scenery of the Campagna about Rome, Monti Cavo, the summit, rising above an amphitheatre of magnificent woods, to an elevation of 2965 French feet. The view is very extensive: below is the lake of Albano, the finest of the volcanic lakes in Italy, and the modern town of the same name. Few traces remain of Alba Longa, the ancient capital of Latium.

[472] On the summit of the Alban Mount, on the site of the present convent, stood the temple of Jupiter Latialis, where the Latin tribes assembled annually, and renewed their league, during the

Feriae Latinae, instituted by Tarquinus Superbus. It was here, also, that Roman generals, who were refused the honours of a full triumph, performed the ovation, and sacrificed to Jupiter Latialis. Part of the triumphal way by which the mountain was ascended, formed of vast blocks of lava, is still in good preservation, leading through groves of chestnut trees of vast size and age. Spanning them with extended arms—none of the shortest—the operation was repeated five times in compassing their girth.

[473] CALIGULA. See c. v. of his life.

[474] A.U.C. 793. Life of CALIGULA, cc. xliv., xlv., etc.

[475] A.U.C. 794.

[476] The chamber of Mercury; the names of deities being given to different apartments, as those "of Isis," "of the Muses," etc.

[477] See the note, p. 265.

[478] The attentive reader will have marked the gradual growth of the power of the pretorian guard, who now, and on so many future occasions, ruled the destinies of the empire.

[479] See AUGUSTUS, cc. xliii., xlv.

[480] Ib. c. ci.

[481] Germanicus.

[482] Naples and other cities on that coast were Greek colonies.

[483] This arch was erected in memory of the standards (the eagles) lost by Varus, in Germany, having been recovered by Germanicus under the auspices of Tiberius. See his Life, c. xlvii.; and Tacit. Annal. ii. 41. It seems to have stood at the foot of the Capitol, on the side of the Forum, near the temple of Concord; but there are no remains of it.

[484] Tacitus informs us that the same application had been made by Tiberius. Annal. iii. The prefect of the pretorian guards, high and important as his office had now become, was not allowed to enter the senate-house, unless he belonged to the equestrian order.

[485] The procurators had the administration of some of the less important provinces, with rank and authority inferior to that of the

pro- consuls and prefects. Frequent mention of these officers is made by Josephus; and Pontius Pilate, who sentenced our Lord to crucifixion, held that office in Judaea, under Tiberius.

[486] Pollio and Messala were distinguished orators, who flourished under the Caesars Julius and Augustus.

[487] A.U.C. 795, 796.

[488] A.U.C. 800, 804.

[489] "Ad bestias" had become a new and frequent sentence for malefactors. It will be recollected, that it was the most usual form of martyrdom for the primitive Christians. Polycarp was brought all the way from Smyrna to be exposed to it in the amphitheatre at Rome.

[490] This reminds us of the decision of Solomon in the case of the two mothers, who each claimed a child as their own, 1 Kings iii. 22-27.

[491] A most absurd judicial conclusion, the business of the judge or court being to decide, on weighing the evidence, on which side the truth preponderated.

[492] See the note in CALIGULA, c. xix., as to Suetonius's sources of information from persons cotemporary with the occurrences he relates.

[493] The insult was conveyed in Greek, which seems, from Suetonius, to have been in very common use at Rome: kai su geron ei, kai moros.

[494] A.U.C. 798, or 800.

[495] There was a proverb to the same effect: "Si non caste, saltem caute."

[496] Ptolemy appointed him to an office which led him to assume a foreign dress. Rabirius was defended by Cicero in one of his orations, which is extant.

[497] The Sigillaria was a street in Rome, where a fair was held after the Saturnalia, which lasted seven days; and toys, consisting of little images and dolls, which gave their name to the street and fes-

tival, were sold. It appears from the text, that other articles were exposed for sale in this street. Among these were included elegant vases of silver and bronze. There appears also to have been a bookseller's shop, for an ancient writer tells us that a friend of his showed him a copy of the Second Book of the Aeneid, which he had purchased there.

[498] Opposed to this statement there is a passage in Servius Georgius, iii. 37, asserting that he had heard (accipimus) that Augustus, besides his victories in the east, triumphed over the Britons in the west; and Horace says:—

Augustus adjectis Britannis
Imperio gravibusque Persis.—Ode iii. 5, 1.

Strabo likewise informs us, that in his time, the petty British kings sent embassies to cultivate the alliance of Augustus, and make offerings in the Capitol: and that nearly the whole island was on terms of amity with the Romans, and, as well as the Gauls, paid a light tribute.— Strabo, B. iv. p. 138.

That Augustus contemplated a descent on the island, but was prevented from attempting it by his being recalled from Gaul by the disturbances in Dalmatia, is very probable. Horace offers his vows for its success:

Serves iturum, Caesarem in ultimos Orbis Britannos.—Ode i. 35.

But the word iturus shews that the scheme was only projected, and the lines previously quoted are mere poetical flattery. Strabo's statement of the communications kept up with the petty kings of Britain, who were perhaps divided by intestine wars, are, to a certain extent, probably correct, as such a policy would be a prelude to the intended expedition.

[499] Circius. Aulus Gellius, Seneca, and Pliny, mention under this name the strong southerly gales which prevail in the gulf of Genoa and the neighbouring seas.

[500] The Stoechades were the islands now called Hieres, off Toulon.

[501] Claudius must have expended more time in his march from Marseilles to Gessoriacum, as Boulogne was then called, than in his vaunted conquest of Britain.

[502] In point of fact, he was only sixteen days in the island, receiving the submission of some tribes in the south-eastern districts. But the way had been prepared for him by his able general, Aulus Plautius, who defeated Cunobeline, and made himself master of his capital, Camulodunum, or Colchester. These successes were followed up by Ostorius, who conquered Caractacus and sent him to Rome.

It is singular that Suetonius has supplied us with no particulars of these events. Some account of them is given in the disquisition appended to this life of CLAUDIUS.

The expedition of Plautius took place A.U.C. 796., A.D. 44.

[503] Carpentum: see note in CALIGULA, c. xv.

[504] The Aemiliana, so called because it contained the monuments of the family of that name, was a suburb of Rome, on the Via Lata, outside the gate.

[505] The Diribitorium was a house in the Flaminian Circus, begun by Agrippa, and finished by Augustus, in which soldiers were mustered and their pay distributed, from whence it derived its name. When the Romans went to give their votes at the election of magistrates, they were conducted by officers named Diribitores. It is possible that one and the same building may have been used for both purposes.

The Flaminian Circus was without the city walls, in the Campus Martius.
The Roman college now stands on its site.

[506] A law brought in by the consuls Papius Mutilus and Quintus Poppaeus; respecting which, see AUGUSTUS, c. xxxiv.

[507] The Fucine Lake is now called Lago di Celano, in the Farther Abruzzi. It is very extensive, but shallow, so that the difficulty of constructing the Claudian emissary, can scarcely be compared to

that encountered in a similar work for lowering the level of the waters in the Alban lake, completed A.U.C. 359.

[508] Respecting the Claudian aqueduct, see CALIGULA, c. xxi.

[509] Ostia is referred to in a note, TIBERIUS, c. xi.

[510] Suetonius calls this "the great obelisk" in comparison with those which Augustus had placed in the Circus Maximus and Campus Martius. The one here mentioned was erected by Caligula in his Circus, afterwards called the Circus of Nero. It stood at Heliopolis, having been dedicated to the sun, as Herodotus informs us, by Phero, son of Sesostris, in acknowledgment of his recovery from blindness. It was removed by Pope Sixtus V. in 1586, under the celebrated architect, Fontana, to the centre of the area before St. Peter's, in the Vatican, not far from its former position. This obelisk is a solid piece of red granite, without hieroglyphics, and, with the pedestal and ornaments at the top, is 182 feet high. The height of the obelisk itself is 113 palms, or 84 feet.

[511] Pliny relates some curious particulars of this ship: "A fir tree of prodigious size was used in the vessel which, by the command of Caligula, brought the obelisk from Egypt, which stands in the Vatican Circus, and four blocks of the same sort of stone to support it. Nothing certainly ever appeared on the sea more astonishing than this vessel; 120,000 bushels of lentiles served for its ballast; the length of it nearly equalled all the left side of the port of Ostia; for it was sent there by the emperor Claudius. The thickness of the tree was as much as four men could embrace with their arms."—B. xvi. c. 76.

[512] See AUGUSTUS, c. xxxi. It appears to have been often a prey to the flames, TIBERIUS, c. xli.; CALIGULA, c. xx.

[513] Contrary to the usual custom of rising and saluting the emperor without acclamations.

[514] A.U.C. 800.

[515] The Secular Games had been celebrated by Augustus, A.U.C. 736. See c. xxxi. of his life, and the Epode of Horace written on the occasion.

[516] In the circus which he had himself built.

[517] Tophina; Tuffo, a porous stone of volcanic origin, which abounds in the neighbourhood of Rome, and, with the Travertino, is employed in all common buildings.

[518] In compliment to the troops to whom he owed his elevation: see before, c. xi.

[519] Palumbus was a gladiator: and Claudius condescended to pun upon his name, which signifies a wood-pigeon.

[520] See before, c. xvii. Described is c. xx and note.

[521] See before, AUGUSTUS, c. xxxiv.

[522] To reward his able services as commander of the army in Britain. See before, c. xvii.

[523] German tribes between the Elbe and the Weser, whose chief seat was at Bremen, and others about Ems or Lueneburg.

[524] This island in the Tiber, opposite the Campus Martius, is said to have been formed by the corn sown by Tarquin the Proud on that consecrated field, and cut down and thrown by order of the consuls into the river. The water being low, it lodged in the bed of the stream, and gradual deposits of mud raising it above the level of the water, it was in course of time covered with buildings. Among these was the temple of Aesculapius, erected A.U.C. 462, to receive the serpent, the emblem of that deity which was brought to Rome in the time of a plague. There is a coin of Antoninus Pius recording this event, and Lumisdus has preserved copies of some curious votive inscriptions in acknowledgment of cures which were found in its ruins, Antiquities of Rome, p. 379.

It was common for the patient after having been exposed some nights in the temple, without being cured, to depart and put an end to his life. Suetonius here informs us that slaves so exposed, at least obtained their freedom.

[525] Which were carried on the shoulders of slaves. This prohibition had for its object either to save the wear and tear in the narrow streets, or to pay respect to the liberties of the town.

[526] See the note in c. i. of this life of CLAUDIUS.

[527] Seleucus Philopater, son of Antiochus the Great, who being conquered by the Romans, the succeeding kings of Syria acknowledged the supremacy of Rome.

[528] Suetonius has already, in TIBERIUS, c. xxxvi., mentioned the expulsion of the Jews from Rome, and this passage confirms the conjecture, offered in the note, that the Christians were obscurely alluded to in the former notice. The antagonism between Christianity and Judaism appears to have given rise to the tumults which first led the authorities to interfere. Thus much we seem to learn from both passages: but the most enlightened men of that age were singularly ill-informed on the stupendous events which had recently occurred in Judaea, and we find Suetonius, although he lived at the commencement of the first century of the Christian aera, when the memory of these occurrences was still fresh, and it might be supposed, by that time, widely diffused, transplanting Christ from Jerusalem to Rome, and placing him in the time of Claudius, although the crucifixion took place during the reign of Tiberius.

St. Luke, Acts xviii. 2, mentions the expulsion of the Jews from Rome by the emperor Claudius: Dio, however, says that he did not expel them, but only forbad their religious assemblies.

It was very natural for Suetonius to write Chrestus instead of Christus, as the former was a name in use among the Greeks and Romans. Among others, Cicero mentions a person of that name in his Fam. Ep. 11. 8.

[529] Pliny tells us that Druidism had its origin in Gaul, and was transplanted into Britain, xxi. 1. Julius Caesar asserts just the contrary, Bell. Gall. vi. 13, 11. The edict of Claudius was not carried into effect; at least, we find vestiges of Druidism in Gaul, during the reigns of Nero and Alexander Severus.

[530] The Eleusinian mysteries were never transferred from Athens to Rome, notwithstanding this attempt of Claudius, and although Aurelius Victor says that Adrian effected it.

[531] A.U.C. 801.

[532] A.U.C. 773.

[533] It would seem from this passage, that the cognomen of "the Great," had now been restored to the descendants of Cneius Pompey, on whom it was first conferred.

[534] A.U.C. 806.

[535] A.U.C. 803.

[536] This is the Felix mentioned in the Acts, cc. xxiii. and xxiv., before whom St. Paul pleaded. He is mentioned by Josephus; and Tacitus, who calls him Felix Antonius, gives his character: Annal. v, 9. 6.

[537] It appears that two of these wives of Felix were named Drusilla. One, mentioned Acts xxiv. 24, and there called a Jewess, was the sister of king Agrippa, and had married before, Azizus, king of the Emessenes. The other Drusilla, though not a queen, was of royal birth, being the granddaughter of Cleopatra by Mark Antony. Who the third wife of Felix was, is unknown.

[538] Tacitus and Josephus mention that Pallas was the brother of Felix, and the younger Pliny ridicules the pompous inscription on his tomb.

[539] A.U.C. 802.

[540] The Salii, the priests of Mars, twelve in number, were instituted by Numa. Their dress was an embroidered tunic, bound with a girdle ornamented with brass. They wore on their head a conical cap, of a considerable height; carried a sword by their side; in their right hand a spear or rod, and in their left, one of the Ancilia, or shields of Mars. On solemn occasions, they used to go to the Capitol, through the Forum and other public parts of the city, dancing and singing sacred songs, said to have been composed by Numa; which, in the time of Horace, could hardly be understood by any one, even the priests themselves. The most solemn procession of the Salii was on the first of March, in commemoration of the time when the sacred shield was believed to have fallen from heaven, in the

reign of Numa. After their procession, they had a splendid entertainment, the luxury of which was proverbial.

[541] Scaliger and Casauhon give Teleggenius as the reading of the best manuscripts. Whoever he was, his name seems to have been a bye-word for a notorious fool.

[542] Titus Livius, the prince of Roman historians, died in the fourth year of the reign of Tiberius, A.U.C. 771; at which time Claudius was about twenty-seven years old, having been born A.U.C. 744.

[543] Asinius Gallus was the son of Asinius Pollio, the famous orator, and had written a hook comparing his father with Cicero, and giving the former the preference.

[544] Quintilian informs us, that one of the three new letters the emperor Claudius attempted to introduce, was the Aeolic digamma, which had the same force as v consonant. Priscian calls another antisigns, and says that the character proposed was two Greek sigmas, back to back, and that it was substituted for the Greek ps. The other letter is not known, and all three soon fell into disuse.

[545] Caesar by birth, not by adoption, as the preceding emperors had been, and as Nero would be, if he succeeded.

[546] Tacitus informs us, that the poison was prepared by Locusta, of whom we shall hear, NERO, c. xxxiii. etc.

[547] A.U.C. 806; A.D. 54.